Fast Company

by Carla Ching

FOR PRODUCTION INQUIRIES

UNITED KINGDOM AND EUROPE
licensing@concordtheatricals.co.uk
020-7054-7298

UNITED STATES AND CANADA
info@concordtheatricals.com
1-866-979-0447

Each title is subject to availability from Concord Theatricals Corp., depending upon country of performance. Please be aware that *FAST COMPANY* may not be licensed by Concord Theatricals Corp. in your territory. Professional and amateur producers should contact the nearest Concord Theatricals Corp. office or licensing partner to verify availability.

No one shall make any changes in this title(s) for the purpose of production. No part of this book may be reproduced, stored in a retrieval system, scanned, uploaded, or transmitted in any form, by any means, now known or yet to be invented, including mechanical, electronic, digital, photocopying, recording, videotaping, or otherwise, without the prior written permission of the publisher. No one shall share this title(s), or any part of this title(s), through any social media or file hosting websites.

For all inquiries regarding motion picture, television, online/digital and other media rights, please contact Concord Theatricals Corp.

MUSIC AND THIRD-PARTY MATERIALS USE NOTE

Licensees are solely responsible for obtaining formal written permission from copyright owners to use copyrighted music and/or other copyrighted third-party materials (e.g. artworks, logos) in the performance of this play and are strongly cautioned to do so. If no such permission is obtained by the licensee, then the licensee must use only original music and materials that the licensee owns and controls. Licensees are solely responsible and liable for clearances of all third-party copyrighted materials, including without limitation music, and shall indemnify the copyright owners of the play(s) and their licensing agent, Concord Theatricals Corp., against any costs, expenses, losses and liabilities arising from the use of such copyrighted third-party materials by licensees. For music, please contact the appropriate music licensing authority in your territory for the rights to any incidental music.

IMPORTANT BILLING AND CREDIT REQUIREMENTS

If you have obtained performance rights to this title, please refer to your licensing agreement for important billing and credit requirements.

FAST COMPANY was commissioned and developed by the Ensemble Studio Theatre/Alfred P. Sloan Foundation Science and Technology Project and received its New York premiere on March 17, 2014.

It was workshopped and developed in the 2013 Pacific Playwrights Festival at South Coast Repertory and originally produced by South Coast Repertory on October 11, 2013.

FAST COMPANY was first produced by South Coast Repertory Theatre (Mark Masterson, Artistic Director; Paula Tomei, Managing Director) in Costa Mesa, California on October 11, 2013. The production was directed by Bart DeLorenzo with dramaturgy by Kelly Miller, scenic design by Keith Mitchell, lighting design by Tom Ontiveros, costume design by Ann Closs-Farley, original music and soundscape by John Ballinger, projection design by Jason H. Thompson, fight consultation by Ken Merckx, and magic consultation by Alfonso Aceituno. The Production Manager was Joshua Marchesi and the Production Stage Manager was Jennifer Ellen Butler. The cast was as follows:

BLUE . . . . Jackie Chung

FRANCIS . . . . .Lawrence Kao

H . . . . Nelson Lee

MABLE . . . . Emily Kuroda

FAST COMPANY was originally an EST/Sloan commission and a revised version was produced by Ensemble Studio Theatre (William Carden, Artistic Director; Paul Slee, Executive Director; Graeme Gillis, Associate Artistic Director and Program Director of the EST/Sloan Project) in New York City on March 17, 2014. The production was directed by Robert Ross Parker with dramaturgy by Linsay Firman, scenic and lighting design by Nick Francone, costume design by Suzanne Chesney, props design by Travis Bell, sound design and original music by Shane Rettig, fight choreography by Michael Chin, magic consultation by Ruy Iskandar, and science advisement from Gabriel Cwilich and Qingmin Liu. The Production Manager was Joe Lankheet and the Production Stage Manager was Rebecca McBee. The cast was as follows:

BLUE. . . . . Stephanie Hsu

FRANCIS . . . . .Christopher Larkin

H . . . . Moses Villarama

MABLE . . . . .Mia Katigbak

CHARACTERS

An Asian American Family

BLUE, early to mid 20s – the Ivy League student
FRANCIS, mid to late 20s – the magician
H, late 20s to early 30s – the sports writer
MABLE, 55 to 60 – the con man

SETTING

New York City
Rio de Janeiro
Providence, Rhode Island
Hollywood, California

AUTHOR'S NOTES

– indicates a cut-off
… indicates a beat or trail off
/ indicates an overlap in dialogue

For Chritopher

Scene One
Pig-In-A-Poke

*(In an art gallery in New York, **BLUE** pores over glass cases containing rare comic books. **H** loosens his tie. She peers at the array of comics, lit like diamonds.)*

BLUE. *Fantastic Four #1. The Amazing Spider-Man. The Incredible Hulk.*

> *(**H** opens the glass case with two keys. He reaches in and pulls out the* Fantastic Four. *Hands it to* **BLUE** *who holds it up to the light in its plastic sleeve.)*

Your fabrication work is getting better.

H. Excuse me, my fabrication work has always been *awesome*.

BLUE. Frankie told me about the Ai Weiwei vase copies you made for the Mexico City job.

H. That was not my fault.

BLUE. The mark picked them up to see what her half mill was buying and the wet paint ended up all over her hands, her fur coat, her wig. Blew the whole job.

H. It was raining. Stupid humidity kept the paint from drying.

BLUE. Lucky for you, there's no rain in the forecast today. So…where is she?

H. I believe what you're looking for is over here.

> *(He goes over and uses the two keys around his neck to unlock a specially lit case.)*

BLUE. *Action Comics #1.* Superman's first appearance in the comic sphere –

> *(She picks it up.)*

BLUE. *(cont.)* 1.5 million feels good in my hands.

> (**H** *pulls out a second comic from under the counter.*)

H. That one's only worth about $8.16 plus tax. Your million dollar baby is over here.

> (*He hands the second comic to* **BLUE.** *She looks at them side by side.*)

BLUE. That's fucking incredible.

H. Can you tell them apart?

BLUE. No.

H. So what was that about my fabrication skills?

> (*She looks at each one and compares them.*)

BLUE. Okay. It's kind of awesome –

H. Kind of? Look at the slight fold on the cover. And the barely perceptible color bleed on the corner of the title. Just like the original.

BLUE. She's perfect.

H. Almost. Ink saturation. True paper degradation. There are some things I can't fake. It looks great till you take a magnifying glass to it. And this guy has a trained eye. So, make sure you show him the real one, get the signature of sale and the money before swapping in the copy.

BLUE. Right.

H. Now, run through it. I'll be The Mark. Remember the points to hit –

BLUE. Flattery. Flirtation. Misdirection.

> (**BLUE** *puts the original in the display case, the copy under the counter.* **H** *transforms himself into "The Mark": a young, super wealthy, Asiaphile comic collector. Stretches his hand out in introduction.*)

H. *(as The Mark)* Ms. Wong. *(in Cantonese)* Néih hóu ma?

BLUE. *(as Ms. Wong, in a flawless Hong Kong accent)* Mr. Jamison. Your Cantonese is excellent.

H. I've traveled all throughout Asia. I love all things Asian.

BLUE. *(falling out of role)* Gross!

H. He's an Asiaphile. And rich and entitled. You have to be prepared for anything.

BLUE. *(back in role)* I'd love to hear all about your travels sometime.

H. Perhaps over drinks tonight?

BLUE. Perhaps. But first…

> (**BLUE** *takes out the original copy of the comic.*)

I am proud to present *Action Comics #1*. Rated as 9.0 Condition, by the Certified Guarantee Company. You have exquisite taste.

H. Can I? Touch it?

BLUE. Of course.

> (**H** *uses a jeweler's eye piece to examine the comic carefully.*)

H. Just gorgeous. Ink's good. Paper's good. And you have the certificate of authenticity?

> (*He uses an ultraviolet light to scan the certificate.*)

BLUE. You'll notice the CGC seal and barcode right there.

H. Good. Let's consider this bad boy bought so we can move onto…other things. Where do I sign?

BLUE. Here, here and here.

> (*She closes the case so they have a surface to write on. Presents him with papers and a pen. While he is busy fumbling with papers, she slips out the copy and holds it in front of the original.*)

[Projection: The Swap]

> (*Freeze for a moment on* **BLUE** *pulling the switch. Clunk!* **BLUE** *drops the original into her bag and stands holding the copy in front of* **H.***)*

H. *(out of role)* You better practice that drop.

BLUE. *(out of role)* Shut up.

(*He signs. Hands her a briefcase of money.*)

Pleasure doing business with you.

(*She hands the fake comic to* **H.**)

H. The pleasure is all mine.

FRANCIS. *(offstage)* So you were going to slip him the copy. And keep the original. Classic Pig-In-A-Poke.

(**H** *freezes.*)

BLUE. That was the plan.

(*Lights up on* **FRANCIS**' *Laboratory of Magic in Hollywood, California. The walls are lined with books on magic. An architect's table might hold plans and notes in code. In the middle of it all is a pillar of ice, upon which leans* **FRANCIS**.)

FRANCIS. You were Inside Man? I heard you've been playing The Lure.

BLUE. I've moved up.

FRANCIS. Good, because nobody respects –

BLUE. I moved up.

FRANCIS. Well, it was a good set-up. So, what went wrong?

BLUE. It went according to plan. Except when I went to show the mark the original, it was gone.

FRANCIS. What happened to it?

BLUE. One of my guys…

(**FRANCIS** *looks at her: What? Spit it out.*)

One of my guys stole it.

FRANCIS. One of *your guys* stole it?

(**FRANCIS** *starts laughing.*)

You let someone steal from you on a job you were running? What kind of con man are you?

BLUE. Like you've never made a mistake before.

FRANCIS. Not like this! Not a 1.5 million dollar mistake.

*(**BLUE** gives him the look of death and paces.)*

If you're running a crew, you have to know if something feels wrong.

BLUE. I'm not in a place to be lectured –

FRANCIS. Wrong with The Mark, wrong with the team. If the *air's* a degree too warm, you have to know –

BLUE. I know.

FRANCIS. All you have is your gut, fast hands and faster thinking. Hands and thinking, you can learn. But if you don't have the gut –

BLUE. I have the gut.

FRANCIS. Do you?

BLUE. …

FRANCIS. Start at the beginning. Don't leave anything out.

BLUE. Okay, but if you start being all judgy and shit, I'm not talking anymore.

FRANCIS. If you didn't fuck up, I wouldn't have to be judgy.

*(**BLUE** slaps her hand over her mouth.)*

That was cute when you were six, but now it's just sad.

*(**BLUE** shrugs.)*

Okay, I won't judge.

*(**BLUE** takes her hand off her mouth.)*

BLUE. Thank you.

FRANCIS. Laugh, I will though. Laugh my ass off.

BLUE. My therapist said I have to learn how to draw lines.

FRANCIS. You're in therapy?

BLUE. I feel hurt sometimes –

FRANCIS. You feel what?

BLUE. I feel hurt when you tell me I've "shit the bed" or "fucked up royally." I need you to use constructive language with me.

FRANCIS. Constructive…*what?*

BLUE. Would it kill you to not be a dick?

FRANCIS. What's the first rule on a job?

BLUE. No feelings.

> (**FRANCIS** *gives her a "See?" look.*)

But we aren't on a job. We're analyzing a job.

FRANCIS. That went wrong. On your watch.

> (**BLUE** *slaps her hand over her mouth.* **FRANCIS** *takes a deep breath.*)

When I say…things that are difficult to hear, I'm just trying to help you.

> (*She pulls her hand off her mouth.*)

BLUE. (*plaintive and earnest*) Just help me without being rude. Please.

FRANCIS. No rudeness. Okay. I can do that… The beginning. I need every detail so we can find where you…

> (**FRANCIS** *catches himself.* **BLUE***'s eyes are on him like lasers.*)

So we can find where…

> (*He chooses his words carefully.*)

Things went wrong.

> (**BLUE** *evil eyes him and goes back to the beginning, pacing.*)

BLUE. Do you know who Jason Manheim is?

FRANCIS. The guy in the exploding helicopter movies?

> (**BLUE** *nods.*)

I heard he's a real nut job.

BLUE. He's…complicated.

FRANCIS. I heard he collects guns. Has these former Hong Kong Triad as his security team.

BLUE. All those things are true. You add that to him having a nasty temper and he's a guy you don't want to fuck with.

FRANCIS. Tell me you didn't.

BLUE. …

FRANCIS. Blue!

BLUE. I wouldn't have except he's also a big comic nerd. He has a really valuable collection and the crown jewel of it is *Action Comics #1.*

FRANCIS. What's that?

BLUE. The first comic Superman ever appears in. There are only ten copies in good condition worldwide and Manheim has the best one.

FRANCIS. How do you know all this?

BLUE. We might've dated. For a second.

(*Before* **FRANCIS** *can protest –*)

You said. No judging.

(**FRANCIS** *just shakes his head at her.*)

This weekend is the Oscars, so we knew he'd be in LA and this would be our chance to steal it. Jason has his whole comic collection on display in his office. High security frames. So, we were gonna boost the original *Action Comics #1,* sell it to The Mark, and then pull a Pig-In-A-Poke –

FRANCIS. Swapping the original for a copy and sending the buyer home with the fake.

BLUE. Then we'd return Jason's original to his office and he'd be none the wiser. In and out. Clean.

FRANCIS. So you were just borrowing it?

BLUE. Right. Just a borrow.

FRANCIS. Who was The Mark?

BLUE. A douchebag trust fund collector.

FRANCIS. Who roped him?

BLUE. Redheaded Johnny.

FRANCIS. I hate that guy. He cheats at cards.

BLUE. Who do we know who doesn't cheat at cards?

(**FRANCIS** *gives her a look.*)

The rest of us have to cheat. The rest of us aren't as good as you.

FRANCIS. Maybe it was Johnny.

BLUE. If it were, he wouldn't be in the can.

FRANCIS. True. Who else was on the team?

BLUE. Lazy Slade helped set up the store and was driving getaway.

FRANCIS. You used Lazy? Oh, Blue. Why do you think they call him that?

(BLUE *puts her hand over her mouth.*)

Is it Lazy?

BLUE. He got pinched by the cops too.

FRANCIS. They gonna give you up?

BLUE. No.

FRANCIS. How do you know that?

BLUE. They're just not.

FRANCIS. Why, you sleep with them?

(BLUE *gives him a look.*)

Blue!

BLUE. What?

FRANCIS. That doesn't buy you loyalty.

BLUE. I've promised them that their cut is waiting for them when they get out. If they keep it shut.

(FRANCIS *tries to shake off how creeped out he feels.*)

FRANCIS. So then who's left? Roper, Driver, Inside Man… your Fixer. Fixer must have lifted the comic *before* the mark arrived. Who's The Fixer?

BLUE. I'm down one hundred grand in set up, my crew's in the can, I need to get the original back in Manheim's office by Monday morning –

FRANCIS. Who was The Fixer? Find him, find the comic.

BLUE. I'm not in a place to hear "I told you so," I just need you to –

FRANCIS. You didn't fly 2500 miles to play Twenty Questions

BLUE. Frankie, it was H.

(*Beat.* **FRANCIS**' *eyes go wide.*)

FRANCIS. Fucking H was your Fixer? You had a score like this going on and you called H and not me?

BLUE. You said you were out. "Out" means out for most people.

FRANCIS. I am. Out. But H?

BLUE. You always said he was the best Fixer.

FRANCIS. I also told you that you can't trust him farther than you can throw him. Wait. Your whole crew is in jail, right? That isn't an accident. H needed you all out of the way. So he sicced the cops on them.

BLUE. But why didn't he send them after me?

FRANCIS. You can't rule that out. He still might. (*beat*) Can you be tied to the steal at all?

BLUE. Shit.

FRANCIS. What?

BLUE. Fingerprints. H and I went in as maintenance crew to lift it out of his office.

FRANCIS. And you didn't wipe the place down?

BLUE. I was gonna do it when we put the comic back! Oh, shit… Manheim's gonna kill me… He's gonna have his Triad guys kill me –

FRANCIS. No one's going to kill you. If you replace the original before he gets back.

BLUE. But, I don't know where it is! I need a cigarette. Cigarette?

(*She goes for the pack in her hoodie pocket.*)

Dude. Where's my pack?

(*He makes the pack appear out of thin air.*)

FRANCIS. What, these? Misdirection, B. You're getting slow.

(*She takes out a cigarette. Lights it.*)

BLUE. He broke code. You never turn on your own crew. Why would he do that, Frankie?

FRANCIS. Go back. Think. Were there any other clues?

> (*Lights shift to the gallery. The sound of a rewinding tape and* H *and* BLUE *are back looking at the comic.*)

H. Look at the slight fold on the cover. And the barely perceptible color bleed –

FRANCIS. Yeah, I got all that. Anything else?

BLUE. Well, later, he said –

H. You know, you're talented. And this job could make you. No more rinky-dink jobs in B-market towns –

FRANCIS. (*offstage*) Stop. Where's he looking?

> (H *freezes.* FRANCIS *walks into the gallery.*)

BLUE. Left.

FRANCIS. Looking right is generally conjuring a memory, remembering something true. Upper left quadrant means he's inventing…making shit up. He doesn't believe a word he's saying.

BLUE. That I'm talented or that this job could make me?

FRANCIS. Probably both. Think like a Roper. What else do you see?

> (BLUE *scans* H.)

BLUE. I don't know. He's gained a little weight.

FRANCIS. What else?

BLUE. Bags under the eyes. He hasn't been sleeping.

FRANCIS. Good. Also, the weight and the sallow skin says he's eating junk.

BLUE. Which he does when he's depressed. Spaghetti-Os. Peanut butter straight from the jar. And…his nails are bitten down. Oh, shit.

FRANCIS. And when does he bite his nails?

BLUE. Shit. Shit shit shit shit shit. Goddamnit!

> (*Lights down on* H.)

FRANCIS. Homework, B. Before every job, you get the full run down on the whole crew. How much they have in the bank, their rep on other crews, their predilection for coke or prostitutes. Anything that makes them a liability.

BLUE. But he's our fucking brother!

FRANCIS. Especially because he's our brother! Strike that. My mom shacking up with your dad doesn't make that sack of shit my brother.

BLUE. Not even in a *Brady Bunch* way?

FRANCIS. Not even.

BLUE. So, I'm not your sister, then?

FRANCIS. You're different.

BLUE. Am I?

(**FRANCIS** *considers her carefully.*)

FRANCIS. Yes, and because you are, I'm telling you: Never. Trust. Anyone.

BLUE. Even you?

FRANCIS. Even me.

(*beat*)

If you ran the check, you'd know he's in to Jimmy for quite a bit of money.

BLUE. He swore to me he was clean! I specifically asked him –

FRANCIS. A grifter is always grifting. And a gambler's always gambling. He came to me a month ago. Asked for a loan.

BLUE. You should've told me.

FRANCIS. You should've asked.

(**BLUE**'s *crushed. She should have known better.*)

BLUE. You give him any money?

FRANCIS. If I did, would we be here?

(**BLUE** *paces.*)

So, if he's into Jimmy for that much and has no cash flow –

BLUE. He's gonna try to liquidate and make tracks.

FRANCIS. 10 to 1, yes.

BLUE. Help me get it back? Before H disappears.

FRANCIS. I can't.

BLUE. Why?

FRANCIS. I have a thing.

BLUE. A thing?

FRANCIS. The day after tomorrow.

BLUE. Move it.

FRANCIS. Can't. It's a live TV appearance.

BLUE. Card tricks actually paying the bills?

FRANCIS. Card *effects*. And no, it's not cards.

BLUE. Then, what? Walking through fire? Locking yourself in a refrigerator? *(beat)* Oh, my god, are you locking yourself in a refrigerator?

FRANCIS. It's a pillar made of ice.

BLUE. What?

> *(He waves grandly towards the ice pillar, goes up and sits inside.)*

FRANCIS. It's part of a *Dateline* special on Magic in relation to perception and cognition. I'm gonna sit in a pillar of ice for three days –

BLUE. Close-up magic with cards and coins, fine. But, the carnival sideshow endurance bullshit –

FRANCIS. Whatever, you don't understand. You've never tried to understand why I –

BLUE. Why you walked away from something you were truly gifted at. No, I don't. Some of us have to work at it. Work hard. And you just…piss it away.

FRANCIS. I don't like the life. Or the company.

> *(**BLUE** takes this as a slap to the face. She starts gathering her things.)*

BLUE. I shouldn't have come here. It's my fuck up. My responsibility. I'll fix it.

FRANCIS. Good.

(As **BLUE** *makes for the door –)*

BLUE. Maybe I'll hire The Dentist to find H.

(And she's gone. **FRANCIS** *calls after her.)*

FRANCIS. You'll what?

(She reappears.)

BLUE. You heard of him? Young guy who extracts the truth out of liars. Recovers missing things from thieves. Extremely effective. He's a gun for hire. I'll hire him.

FRANCIS. B. You heard what he does to people?

BLUE. I've heard what he does. I'll hire The Dentist to go to work on H until he gives it up.

FRANCIS. That guy is an animal. You do not want to go down that road –

BLUE. You're my first and last ask, Frankie. If you say no, I have to do things the hard way. Help me.

FRANCIS. I don't like what this work turns me into.

BLUE. I know. I wouldn't ask if I had any other way.

FRANCIS. *(beat)* I'll help you on one condition.

BLUE. Anything.

FRANCIS. You get out of all this.

BLUE. *(crushed)* Anything except that.

FRANCIS. This is the *last* con.

BLUE. Frankie, I'm good at this. It's the biggest job anybody's pulled in the last three years.

FRANCIS. And you screwed it up.

BLUE. If we get it back –

FRANCIS. You can retire a legend.

BLUE. Frankie!

FRANCIS. Find another angle. Find something else you're good at. I've seen people sell themselves off piece by piece in this business. Before they even realize they've sold everything.

BLUE. I'm not like you.

FRANCIS. You want my help? This is the last job.

BLUE. What if we don't get it?

FRANCIS. Then, I won't stand in your way. But if we get it, this is the last one. Say it.

> (**BLUE** *tries to think of any counter, but she's out of moves.*)

BLUE. Jesus. If we get it back…

FRANCIS. This is the last one.

BLUE. *(mumbling)* This is…the last one.

FRANCIS. Mean it.

BLUE. I mean it!

FRANCIS. Good. *(beat)* So, I have an idea.

> (**BLUE** *leans in conspiratorially.*)

BLUE. Yes?

FRANCIS. You're not gonna like it –

BLUE. What?

FRANCIS. *(beat)* We're gonna have to call Mable.

BLUE. No. N-O. Big no.

FRANCIS. I can rope him.

BLUE. I can be The Fixer. Do the set-up.

FRANCIS. But for the rest of it, to plan it? To find the right angle to rope H? We're going to need Mable.

BLUE. She'll undermine me.

FRANCIS. It's your crew. Run it. *(beat)* Look, this is your mess. If you have a better idea of how to clean it up… *(looking at his watch)* Thirty-nine hours and counting…

> (**BLUE** *hems and haws.*)

BLUE. Fine. Call Mable.

> (**FRANCIS** *takes out his phone. Dials.*)

FRANCIS. It's Francis. Yeah, sorry, I've been on the road… Are you in Vegas? No…no, I'm fine, but I'm here with Blue. She's run into a bit of a scrape.

(The sound of screaming on the other end of the line.)

Stop.

*(**FRANCIS** pulls the phone away from his ear. Lets her go on for a second. Then –)*

Are you finished? I'm not doing this on the phone.

(She rails on.)

Mom!

(She finally goes silent.)

How soon can you get here?

*(**BLUE** buries her head in her hands.)*

(Lights.)

Scene Two
Inside Man

*(Lights up on **FRANCIS**' Magic Lab. **BLUE** has her hand over her mouth. **MABLE** is drinking red wine. **FRANCIS** is holding a lit cigarette, watching it burn.)*

MABLE. *(to **BLUE**)* This is why. This is why I didn't teach you. Some have the head for it. Some have the seventh sense. If you don't have either of those, you just end up waist deep in shit.

    *(**MABLE** notices the hand over **BLUE**'s mouth.)*

What are you doing?

FRANCIS. You're being critical.

BLUE. *(forcing her hand down)* My therapist told me I don't have to deal with negativity and criticism, that it's bad for me –

MABLE. Your who?

BLUE. I have to go to therapy because of you!

MABLE. You want me to censor myself?

BLUE. Look, Mable –

MABLE. I didn't come all this way to help you to be told how to act.

FRANCIS. Mable –

    *(**MABLE** downs the rest of the glass.)*

MABLE. Thank you for the wine. I'll see you at Christmas.

    *(**MABLE** picks up her purse and wrap and starts to leave.)*

FRANCIS. *(to **BLUE**)* Do you want him or don't you?

    *(**BLUE** vacillates. Nearly at the door, **MABLE** fumbles with her purse.)*

MABLE. Who stole my cigarettes?

    *(**FRANCIS** produces the cigarettes out of thin air.)*

FRANCIS. You should quit, M. They're bad for you.

(He tosses the pack to her. She continues leaving.)

BLUE. It's a big take, M.

MABLE. *(without turning around)* How much?

BLUE. A mill and a half easy.

MABLE. You had a score this size going on and you didn't call me?

BLUE. Oh, now you want to work with me?

MABLE. What's with the tone? Are you using a tone with me?

BLUE. What is that, huh? You let the boys run on your crew, but you always left me at home. Because I didn't pass your stupid test –

MABLE. The test isn't stupid. The test works –

BLUE. Who leaves a kid on Rockaway Beach? No money, no map. Just "find your way home."

MABLE. Two days. Two days it took you. H did it in three hours. Frankie did it in two –

BLUE. But I got there –

MABLE. Missing both of your mittens and one of your shoes. It was sort of pathetic –

BLUE. I was ten!

MABLE. And here you are again. Fucking up. So are you going to tell me that I was wrong? *(beat)* I was trying to save you from yourself.

BLUE. I learned. On my own. Worked my way up. In a second-tier town. The hard way.

MABLE. Not working any of the respectable roles, but as The Lure? Do you know what kinds of girls play The Lure?

BLUE. I've worked my way up.

MABLE. Who works Boston, anyway? And Providence?

BLUE. I'm in college. It's my cover.

MABLE. *(surprised)* You're in college? What are you studying?

BLUE. Economics.

MABLE. Good. Go be an economist and leave this work to the professionals.

BLUE. I'm not going anywhere. This is *my* job.

MABLE. Maybe. But you're staring down the barrel of the job of the decade and who do you have to invite to dig you out of the hole?

BLUE. Frankie's idea. *Not* mine –

FRANCIS. I said we needed one more –

MABLE. You don't just need one more. You need me. Who else would play Inside Man? *(to* **BLUE***)* You?

BLUE. I am not taking any more shit or any more lip from you, Mable. You are walking into my score, this is my crew.

FRANCIS. B –

(**BLUE** *holds up her hand to quiet* **FRANCIS** *and stays laser focused on* **MABLE***.)*

BLUE. So either behave or take a walk.

MABLE. I could probably do this job in my sleep.

BLUE. Maybe. But I have the intel. And I am cutting you in on it. And I know for a fact that even *you* have never been in on a job this big. So, which is it? You gonna behave, or you gonna walk?

MABLE. Can we dispense with the theatrics and –

BLUE. Mable! Behave or walk?

MABLE. Jesus Christ. It's your crew. I'm just here to play.

(**MABLE** *sits back down and* **FRANCIS** *pours her another glass of wine.)*

Well, you've done your homework, right? He's in to Jimmy for over three hundred grand.

FRANCIS. Three? I thought it was two.

MABLE. If he had just kept away from gambling –

FRANCIS. You had him running jobs in Atlantic City when he was thirteen.

BLUE. Counting cards in Blackjack when he was seventeen. What did you think was gonna happen?

MABLE. You two turned out fine.

(FRANCIS *and* BLUE *exchange looks.*)

FRANCIS. Barely.

MABLE. I told him, only play twenty-one where you can count cards or Hold 'Em where you play the man, not the house. But he had to do sports betting where you have absolutely no control over the outcome.

BLUE. We have to move fast because we think he's going to liquidate and run. And we only have Francis for twenty-four hours.

MABLE. Why?

FRANCIS. I have a thing.

MABLE. You running another job?

BLUE. No. A thing *on TV.*

(FRANCIS *gives* BLUE *the look of death for joyfully blowing up his spot.*)

MABLE. Oh. Still stunting, are we?

FRANCIS. They're not stunts! If you watch this time, then you'll get –

MABLE. Why should I watch you hold your breath in a kiddie pool and call it magic?

FRANCIS. Why should I come home at Christmas and pretend that I like your dried-out turkey? Because it's what you do.

MABLE. So sensitive. You were always so sensitive. That's a liability –

FRANCIS. You're unbelievable –

BLUE. Okay, everybody put your gloves back on. We're working. You put your feelings on hold at work. Right?

(FRANCIS *slumps down dejectedly into a chair.*)

FRANCIS. Right. I am pressing pause on my feelings in the name of business.

BLUE. We need your help taking this asshole down.

MABLE. This is your brother.

BLUE. He's not. He's dead to me.

MABLE. You mean that?

BLUE. I do. Business is business and he broke code. Dead to me.

(**MABLE** *looks at* **BLUE** *with surprise and concern.*)

MABLE. *(beat)* When did you become so cutthroat?

BLUE. When I started running a crew.

FRANCIS. So, what con are we running? We're talking about conning a con artist. It's not going to be easy.

BLUE. I was thinking about this last night. The cons are going the way of the dinosaur.

FRANCIS. What?

MABLE. We use the cons because they always work.

BLUE. No, people have started to get wise. They've been warned about identity theft and Ponzi Schemes. Have you ever Wikipedia'd "Confidence Trick" or "Long Con?" They're all there – The Rag, The Spanish Prisoner, The Pig-In-A-Poke, The Badger Game, The Glim Dropper. All of them.

MABLE. It is harder out there now than it has been. It's true. You really have to look for the dumb ones.

BLUE. So, the question is, how do we get the upper hand? H already knows the cons. He'll see those coming from a mile away. So we need an edge.

MABLE. Like what?

BLUE. I've been doing some reading for school that I think can help.

FRANCIS. For school?

BLUE. I've been reading Game Theory.

MABLE. What's Game Theory?

BLUE. It's a branch of Applied Mathematics –

FRANCIS. I hate math.

BLUE. If life is a game, it shows you how to predict what people are likely to do and act accordingly to win. Like right now. I predicted Francis would balk because he hates math.

FRANCIS. I do. I hate math.

BLUE. So, Francis thinks if he's grouchy enough –

FRANCIS. Stop wasting my time. Can we just pick a con?

BLUE. I'll take him on like I usually do and this will devolve into an insult contest –

FRANCIS. Thinking isn't your strong point, why don't you leave the planning to the professionals?

BLUE. You're not a professional anymore, you left to become a cheesy magician.

FRANCIS. At least I didn't manage to screw up the con of the decade and let 1.5 mill just walk away.

MABLE. Children!

BLUE. *(grabbing ahold of herself)* But instead of calling him an asshole –

FRANCIS. Oh, I'm the asshole?

BLUE. I'll politely ask you to just let me show you.

MABLE. Well, hurry up. Twenty-four hours and counting.

FRANCIS. Mable! You said we run the cons because the cons work –

MABLE. But she's right. We need an edge.

FRANCIS. How are you possibly entertaining –

MABLE. I just want to hear what her plan is. Do you mind?

(**FRANCIS** *throws up his arms and walks away.*)

FRANCIS. *(to BLUE)* You didn't get me.

BLUE. No, but I got Mable. Which was the plan all along.

FRANCIS. What?

BLUE. Watch and learn: we'll start with a classic con set up and then give it a game theory twist. First, Frankie will rope him.

MABLE. Straight rope?

BLUE. Straight rope.

> *(Lights shift. FRANCIS's laboratory melts away. FRANCIS takes out three different cell phones, chooses one and dials.)*

BLUE. Tell him, "The goose flies but the coyote runs."

FRANCIS. Really?

BLUE. That's the code he's using on the market right now.

MABLE. What kind of code is that?

> *(Special up on* **H**, *answering the phone.)*

H. Yeah.

FRANCIS. *(in an Irish accent)* The goose flies but the coyote runs.

> *(***H*** *freezes. Back to* **MABLE** *and* **BLUE.***)*

MABLE. You used that accent on the Vegas Job.

FRANCIS. *(with an Indian accent)* The goose flies but the coyote runs.

MABLE. Kansas City Job.

FRANCIS. *(in a Texan drawl)* The goose flies but the coyote –

MABLE. The Boston Diamond Grab.

FRANCIS. Shit. *(in a Japanese accent)* The goose flies but the coyote –

BLUE. Why are your Asian accents terrible?

FRANCIS. *(trying to do a better Japanese accent)* The goose flies but the coyote –

MABLE. Haven't you learned any new ones?

FRANCIS. No, I've been retired. B – you have a voice modulator on this thing?

BLUE. Yeah. Here.

> *(***FRANCIS*** *plugs his phone into* **BLUE***'s computer. He messes with the pitch of his voice until he sounds like Ving Rhames –)*

FRANCIS. The goose flies but the coyote runs.

H. Every goose I've ever met was a coward.

FRANCIS. That's why you should never trust a goose.

MABLE. Less imposing.

FRANCIS. *(fiddling with the dial until he sounds like Steve Buscemi)* That's why you never trust a goose.

H. How can I help you?

FRANCIS. I have a client who is looking for a rare book. A book that I understand you are in possession of.

H. I already have a buyer.

FRANCIS. He will pay 1.3 million dollars.

H. He is aware that is way below market value.

FRANCIS. He knows. But he also knows it's a stolen commodity. You must be having trouble getting rid of it.

H. The other buyer is a longtime client who is willing to pay market value. 1.5 million. And the fact that it's stolen doesn't bother him.

(**FRANCIS** *covers the mouthpiece.*)

FRANCIS. What's the move?

BLUE. Offer more.

(**MABLE** *gets a better idea.*)

MABLE. No, wait. Offer *less.*

(back to the phone call)

FRANCIS. 1.2 million.

H. You're offering me less?

FRANCIS. I don't believe you have another buyer. And my offer was more than generous. But, I'm feeling less generous by the second. 1.1 million. I could keep going lower. One million dollars –

H. Stop. Stop. One million.

(**H** *sighs.* **FRANCIS** *gives* **MABLE** *a thumbs up.* **BLUE** *is silently pissed that she didn't come up with it.)*

FRANCIS. Wonderful. Let me see when he might be able to meet you.

H. I'm afraid I'm on a bit of a tight timeline.

FRANCIS. Then, how about swinging by my office in Hollywood tomorrow? About 9 pm?

BLUE. You want me to fabricate an office overnight?

(**FRANCIS** *covers the phone.*)

FRANCIS. That a problem for you?

BLUE. Asshole… I'll get it done.

(*back to the phone call*)

FRANCIS. My secretary (*nods over to* **BLUE** *who gives him the finger)* will be in touch with the address.

MABLE. Tell him there will be an authenticator present –

FRANCIS. He'll have an authenticator present, so please bring the book.

H. An authenticator?

(**H** *is bummed. This isn't exactly what he'd planned for. He'd hoped to sell a copy.*)

MABLE. It's the only way we can insure that he brings the real thing and not a copy.

FRANCIS. There are so many copies on the market.

BLUE. Nice.

MABLE. You're welcome.

(**BLUE** *shoots* **MABLE** *a dirty look.*)

FRANCIS. That won't be a problem, will it?

H. No problem at all.

FRANCIS. Perfect. If it all checks out, we'll have ourselves a deal.

H. One million dollars.

FRANCIS. Yes. One million.

H. One more thing. I only work in cash.

FRANCIS. Is there any other way?

(**H** *hangs up. Lights shift.*)

MABLE. So let's say that H has been successfully roped.

FRANCIS. And I get H to that meet. Then what? We'd normally pick a cover. Banker. Billionaire. Art Dealer.

Go in as someone other than us and liberate the mark of the goods. But, he knows all of us.

[Projection: The Con]

BLUE. And we're going to use the fact that *we know him* and *he knows us.* I'll go in…as me.

MABLE. As yourself? We don't do that.

FRANCIS. We always use a cover.

BLUE. It has to be me.

MABLE. Why?

BLUE. A: He'll never see that coming. And B: Only I can leverage what I'm going to tell him. This is the Game Theory part. We run a Psychological Game.

MABLE. A what?

BLUE. We play on the fact that he cares what we think about him. That he wants us to think he's a good guy.

MABLE. How?

*(Special up on **H** holding the briefcase with the comic. **BLUE** walks into the scene with **H**.)*

[Projection: The Psychological Game]

BLUE. *(to **MABLE** and **FRANCIS**)* I'll play his guilt. The fact that we're family. *(to **H**)* You knowingly screwed me over. You're my brother.

H. I know, B. I wish I could take it all back.

BLUE. Then, make it right.

H. How?

BLUE. Give it back, and I forgive you.

H. Really? You'll clear the slate?

BLUE. Yes. All you have to do is give me the comic back.

H. Of course. Here.

*(**H** lifts the briefcase towards **BLUE**.)*

FRANCIS. You think he's gonna just hand it over? Just like that?

*(Lights down on **H**.)*

BLUE. If I do my job right.

FRANCIS. It's risky. We've never run anything like this before. Look, I could do a Pig-In-A-Poke in my sleep. Even get out of a jam if any number of things goes wrong. But a Psychological Game? You don't know the variables, the exit strategies –

BLUE. Do you have a better idea?

FRANCIS. Stick with a classic con: Rent a safe deposit box. Tell him to drop the comic in it, and if it checks out, he'll receive a key to a storage locker where the money is. None of us ever has to show our faces.

MABLE. It's a modified Pig-In-A-Poke.

BLUE. But then the storage locker has no suitcase full of money when he gets there? You really think he's that stupid?

FRANCIS. I think he's desperate. A desperate man becomes very stupid.

MABLE. Blue's crew, her call.

FRANCIS. No. All our necks are out. I want a vote.

BLUE. Fine, but I get two votes because I'm running this.

FRANCIS. Do not!

MABLE. Seems fair. She's running it, so she has twice the risk.

BLUE. They're coming after *me* if we fail. And I have a hundred grand sunk into this thing.

FRANCIS. *(grumbling)* Fine.

BLUE. Two votes for Game Theory. If one of you comes over to my side, I win. Francis?

FRANCIS. Cons.

BLUE. Mable?

MABLE. Hmm…

FRANCIS. Mable. We do the cons because the cons *always* work.

MABLE. Con.

BLUE. Really?

FRANCIS. 2-2. We're tied.

BLUE. Fuck.

MABLE. It's a stalemate.

BLUE. Look, there's a classic tie-breaker that's been used to settle disputes when things were at an impasse. It also happens to be Game Theory.

MABLE. Flip a coin?

BLUE. This is better than that. Because instead of being totally random, we have choice.

> (**BLUE** *raises her fist. They stare at it.*)

MABLE. What the fuck is that?

> (*The rock slowly becomes a sheet of paper. The paper slowly becomes a pair of scissors. The scissors start snipping.*)

FRANCIS. *(incensed)* You want to decide how to get H using Rock-Paper-Scissors?

BLUE. You afraid you'll lose?

FRANCIS. Excuse me. Who beat you at Super Mario Brothers? Chess. Checkers. Monopoly. Poker –

BLUE. Yeah, but –

FRANCIS. Candy Land. Chutes and Ladders. Connect Four. And, lest you forget… Hungry Hungry Hippos.

BLUE. So, play me. What are you afraid of?

> (*She puts out her fist in readiness.*)

FRANCIS. I'm afraid of nothing.

> (*He puts out his fist.* **MABLE** *follows suit.*)

MABLE. I love this game.

BLUE. Ready? On "go." One-Two-Three-Go!

> (*And they do. But* **MABLE** *fucks up and shoots a beat after "Go!"*)

Mable!

FRANCIS. What's so hard to understand about "One-Two-Three-Go?"

MABLE. Sorry.

FRANCIS. You did that so we'd show our hands and you
    could calibrate how you'd shoot in the next round to
    beat us.

MABLE. Did not.

FRANCIS. Did too! You don't think I know your little moves
    after all these –

MABLE. I'm on your team.

FRANCIS. I don't care. You know what? Since you can't play
    fair, you're disqualified –

MABLE. Oh, come on!

FRANCIS. For your cheating ways.

MABLE. But I want to play!

FRANCIS. *(to* MABLE*)* No playing for cheaters! *(to* BLUE*)* You
    and me. Ready?

BLUE. Ready.

FRANCIS. *(to* BLUE*)* On "Go."

> *(They ready their fists.)*

One-Two-Three-Go!

> *(***FRANCIS** *throws rock.* **BLUE** *throws paper. She
> celebrates.)*

Fuck!

BLUE. Psychological Game it is. Set up the meet, Frankie.
    I'm gonna go meet H and get us this comic back.

FRANCIS. Two out of three?

BLUE. No!

> *(Lights.)*

Scene Three
Pigeons and Lambs

(Lights up on a darkened office in Hollywood. A doorbell rings. The sound of the door being buzzed open and **H** *enters.)*

H. I'm sorry I'm late. I got your message about moving the time up, but I –

*(***MABLE*** turns on the lights.)*

MABLE. Hello, Henry.

H. Mable.

MABLE. Surprise.

H. *(beat)* Have you lost weight?

MABLE. Are you losing more hair?

H. Nice to see you too.

MABLE. We missed you at Christmas.

H. Yeah, sorry about that. I had a thing going.

MABLE. You could've called –

H. In South Africa.

MABLE. Were you in jail?

H. Might've been.

MABLE. I suppose you get a pass, then.

*(***H*** looks around. For cameras. For a sign of anyone else.)*

H. So, I gather you've heard.

MABLE. That you broke code, yes. With your sister?

H. I needed big money. Jimmy was threatening to break my knees –

MABLE. Oh, they're always threatening to break your knees –

H. Yeah, and then they do it. You saw what happened to Little Stevie –

MABLE. You never, ever break code. Cross your own crew. All you have is your reputation.

H. This was supposed to be the last one. I was gonna pay off Jimmy and take what's left and move to Costa Rica –

MABLE. Costa Rica?

H. Live in a tree house –

MABLE. A tree house?

H. Be in the middle of nowhere. Away from TVs and the internet and casinos and tracks. Be by myself. Totally alone. It's the only way I can think to stop. And stay stopped.

MABLE. You're finally getting out of gambling?

H. Everything, Mable. I'm getting out of everything.

MABLE. The cons too?

H. Cons too. I was trying to finally go straight.

MABLE. *(incredulous)* Why?

H. I lose more than I win. That's no way to live.

MABLE. So defeatist. That's not the man I raised. I can't believe you want out. You're such a talented Fixer.

> (**H** *side-eyes* **MABLE.**)

H. You always nitpicked every detail of every piece of every job I ever worked on.

MABLE. I never told you how good you were because I didn't want it to go to your head. It's your eye for detail. Your capacity to learn anything –

H. A little about everything. You always said, "A jack of all trades, master of none."

MABLE. I just didn't want you to get overconfident. But, Henry – you're good. The short list of capable Fixers is gonna get a lot shorter if you leave the game.

H. Really?

> (**H** *is genuinely moved by* **MABLE**'s *confirmation of his talents.*)

MABLE. But when you get rattled, you get sloppy. Your Achilles heel. Like just now.

H. What?

MABLE. What is Rule #1 about planning the long con?

H. "Research the Mark."

MABLE. And?

H. When you think you've done enough research, research more. Find every weakness.

MABLE. And in this case, the mark was…

H. We researched Jason Manheim thoroughly –

MABLE. No, dummy. Not on that con. On the other one. Where the mark was your sister.

H. No, wait, they're only the mark if you plan to con them. I didn't plan to take it. Not from the beginning. Jimmy just started coming down on me. Making threats. I was in a corner.

MABLE. And at that point, you forgot to execute Rule #2.

H. "Secure the exit."

MABLE. If you'd written a better exit, you wouldn't have gotten caught. Found an accomplice and blamed it on them. Told her someone stole it from you and sent her on a wild goose chase to find it. So many things. It's like you wanted to get caught.

H. Maybe I did. Because then I'd really be done for good. And I am now, right? Done. A code breaker? No one's gonna work with me now. *(beat)* I'm finally free.

MABLE. Henry, Blue knows it's you. She's called Francis –

H. Francis knows?

MABLE. And they're coming for you.

H. What did they say to you?

MABLE. Blue said that what hurt her is that you were a crew and you did this to her. Even more than your being her brother. She trusted you.

H. She said that?

MABLE. She did.

>(**H** *turns this over in his mind.*)

H. She did not. She's never said that earnest a thing in her whole fucking life.

MABLE. Her words, Henry, not mine. She said if you do this, you're dead to her.

H. *(spooked)* Dead like, she's not talking to me anymore? Or literally dead, like she's gonna put a hit on me?

MABLE. She's thinking about hiring The Dentist.

(**H** *goes pale.*)

H. Jesus Christ.

MABLE. That'd make Jimmy look like a trip to the circus.

H. She wouldn't. Would she? Why would Blue send that animal after me? I'm her brother.

(**H** *paces.*)

MABLE. She says that Jason Manheim's people are onto her. Found her fingerprints on the frame.

H. Goddamnit! I told her to wipe down that frame.

MABLE. If she can't come up with the comic, she's gonna have to run. *(beat)* You really screwed her, Henry.

H. I didn't mean to. I just…didn't know what else to do. Do they know that you're here?

MABLE. *(carefully)* No. I just thought you should know that they're coming for you.

H. If I don't sell it and pay Jimmy…

MABLE. Well, it sounds like you're out of options. So take it and go.

(**H** *looks at* **MABLE**, *surprised. She's gonna let him walk.*)

H. Why does everything I touch turn to shit, M?

MABLE. Some of us never clear the big money, Henry. We can chase it all our lives, but we're not destined for… Costa Rica sounds nice. A tree house sounds nice.

(**MABLE** *starts for the door.*)

H. Mable.

MABLE. Yes?

H. Wait.

> (**MABLE** *turns.*)

Here.

> (**H** *takes the briefcase and slides it over to the other side of the table.* **MABLE** *opens it. Takes out a comic book in a plastic case.*)

MABLE. *Action Comics #1.* This little thing. Causing so much trouble.

H. Give it back to Blue for me?

MABLE. Are you sure?

H. She shouldn't have to run. This is my mess. I'll run.

MABLE. Why don't you give it back to her? You tell her.

H. I'm gonna have to make tracks to dodge Jimmy. I'm gonna have to move fast.

MABLE. Still, you can –

H. Mom. *(beat)* Just, tell her…tell her I'll make it up to her one day.

MABLE. You're sure?

> (**H** *nods.* **MABLE** *takes the comic and slides it in her purse.*)

You have Disappear Money?

H. *(sheepishly)* No.

MABLE. Jesus Christ. You always carry Disappear Money. Just in case.

H. Things have been tight lately.

> (*She reaches inside her bra and pulls out a wad of cash.*)

MABLE. There's about five grand there. That should get you started.

H. *(startled by her gesture)* I can't.

MABLE. Don't be so fucking proud. Take it.

> (**H** *pockets the money and grabs* **MABLE** *in an unexpected hug.*)

H. Thanks, M. I'll get it back to you.

MABLE. Nevermind that.

> *(She breaks the hug, grabs him by the elbows looks him dead in the eye.)*

Keep your head up. And watch your back. Go.

> *(**H** withdraws quickly and moves towards the door.)*

If you see your father out there...

H. Yeah?

MABLE. Tell him to write sometime. *(beat)* And he still owes me ten grand.

> *(**H** smiles furtively and exits out the front door. **MABLE** checks her watch, grabs her purse, and bolts out the front door as well.)*

> *(A minute goes by. **BLUE** arrives through the back door. Picks up her phone and dials.)*

BLUE. Yeah, I'm here. No, not yet, you know he's always late. I'll meet you and Mable at the van when it's done.

> *(She takes her place in the chair and waits. And waits.)*

> *(Lights.)*

Scene Four
Misdirection

*(Lights up on **BLUE** pacing in the office. A special knock at the door. **BLUE** opens the door and **FRANCIS** rushes in.)*

BLUE. I don't understand. Why would H miss the meet? Another buyer?

FRANCIS. No way he could've set up another sale that quick. In cash.

BLUE. You left him a message?

FRANCIS. Two.

BLUE. Call again.

FRANCIS. If we look desperate, he might get spooked.

BLUE. I'm calling Mable.

(She takes out her phone.)

FRANCIS. Really? Something goes wrong and you're gonna call Mommy?

BLUE. Fuck you.

FRANCIS. Look, it's *your* crew, so it's *your* move. So what's the move?

BLUE. I don't know, I need to think.

*(She lights a cigarette. **FRANCIS** steals it.)*

Stop. You're wasting it.

FRANCIS. I'm not. It helps me think.

*(He holds the cigarette, watching it burn. **BLUE** lights a new one. They both study their cigarettes. Thinking.)*

BLUE. I thought I had him dialed. I thought he'd be here.

FRANCIS. …

BLUE. How do I get into his head?

*(**FRANCIS** stubs out his cigarette.)*

FRANCIS. Okay, look. A thousand years ago, Mable said to
    get in the car because we were going somewhere. Just
    her and me. It was a "surprise."
BLUE. Yeah, she said the same shit to me.
FRANCIS. When we ended up at Coney Island,
    I was psyched.
    Cotton Candy. Cyclone.
    And we never got to do anything like that, right?

> *(Coney Island appears behind* **FRANCIS**. *Sounds
> of the Cyclone rollercoaster, pinball machines and
> crowds chattering on the boardwalk.)*

    She told me to get out of the car and empty my pockets.
    I had five bucks and a pack of cards,
    which I handed to her.
    "Okay. Find your way home, Francis."
    She closed the door and drove away.
    My first thought was, "What a bitch."
    The second was, "Alright. I will. I'll get home.
    Because you don't believe that I can."
BLUE. But how'd you do it?
FRANCIS. I scanned the crowd.
    Saw an Asian girl, about my age, eating an ice cream.
    Her jeans were ironed. Her hair was shiny.
    Someone was taking care of her.
    She was standing next to a man
    who looked like her grandfather.
    They were the ones.
BLUE. Your first Marks. What'd you say to them?
FRANCIS. "I think my mother left me here
    because she doesn't want me anymore."
    Then I started bawling
    the minute the words came out of my mouth.
    Fucking embarrassing. Because the girl was cute.
    She handed me a crumpled tissue from her pocket
    to wipe the snot off my face
    and the grandfather asked me for our address.

BLUE. He drove you home? Just like that? Some strange kid?

FRANCIS. Some innocent in a fucked up situation.
Who needed help. That's what he saw.
When we got there, he chewed Mable out.
For leaving a kid on the beach.
For a second I thought she was gonna cry.
It was awesome.

> (*They both enjoy the idea of* **MABLE** *getting schooled.*)

Now, what did I do there?

BLUE. You thought like the girl. And her grandpa. Knew the little things to say to get them to help you. What did they want?

FRANCIS. That's the craziest thing. Their motives were so… pure. Compared to everyone else I knew. They just wanted to help me. And so I used that.

BLUE. How did you know to do all that?

FRANCIS. It's funny. All these things we do by instinct
when we're young.
We don't know what to call them.
We just do them to survive.
Question is, as you get older,
how do you hold onto those instincts and hone them?
Get them to work for you?
(*beat*) You never talked about what happened.
During those three days. Before you got home.

BLUE. Because I don't want to talk about it.

FRANCIS. Did anybody hurt you?

BLUE. It was close, but no.

FRANCIS. Blue –

BLUE. I am not gonna fail in front of her again, so just help me think my way through this. Please?

FRANCIS. (*beat*) Okay. So, think like him. What does he want?

> (*She puts herself in* **H**'s *shoes and thinks like him.*)

BLUE. Not to die.

FRANCIS. Which requires…?

BLUE. Money. Which he could get from the sale of the comic.

FRANCIS. And? What else?

BLUE. …

FRANCIS. Forgiveness. You said it back at my lab.

BLUE. So, either way he'll show. He'll show to sell. Or he'll show to make it right.

FRANCIS. So, don't worry.

(*The doorbell to the office rings.*)

BLUE. Shit. He's here. Hide!

(**FRANCIS** *rushes towards the back entrance stairwell. After* **BLUE***'s sure he's out of sight, she hits the buzzer to open the door and* **MABLE** *walks in with her purse.*)

What are you doing here?

(**FRANCIS** *comes back in.*)

MABLE. (*to* **FRANCIS**) What are you doing here?

FRANCIS. She called me.

MABLE. I finished setting things up at Manheim's to make the switch. I rendezvoused back to the van but you weren't there.

FRANCIS. Why did you just come up here? He could have seen you.

MABLE. I assumed it was done already. He missed the meet? Should we be worried?

(**MABLE** *takes a flask out of her jacket, drops her purse by her feet and drinks.*)

BLUE. No, we thought it through. He'll show up for the money.

FRANCIS. Or forgiveness.

MABLE. Forgiveness?

FRANCIS. *Either way,* he'll show.

MABLE. So, what now?

BLUE. We wait. Maybe his taxi got a flat tire. Maybe he forgot to set his alarm. He'll get here. We'll just be patient.

MABLE. How long do we wait?

BLUE. As long as it takes. He'll call.

MABLE. *(beat)* Call me when he does.

FRANCIS. Why? Where are you going?

MABLE. I have something that I need to take care of Downtown. I'll be back.

FRANCIS. It's one in the morning!

BLUE. Can't it wait?

MABLE. No, darling, it can't. But, like I said, I'm reachable.

FRANCIS. Are you up to something?

MABLE. Why would I be up to something?

FRANCIS. Crew doesn't disperse till the job's done.

(*a tense moment*)

MABLE. Okay. I'll wait.

(*They sit. And wait.* FRANCIS *studies* MABLE.)

I'm really proud of both of you, you know that? You work well together.

(FRANCIS *and* BLUE *are genuinely flattered.*)

FRANCIS. I think that's the first time you've ever said anything nice about my work.

MABLE. Don't let it go to your head.

(*They sit awkwardly. They might all take a drink at the same time. Light a cigarette at the same time.*)

What if he *doesn't* show?

FRANCIS. Then, we'll go to every broke down casino and backwater town that he tries to hole up in, we'll hunt him down, find him and get that comic back.

BLUE. But, that's not gonna happen.

FRANCIS. No, that's not gonna happen.

(MABLE *looks down at the bag in her lap, then looks at* FRANCIS *and* BLUE.)

MABLE. Not. Gonna. Happen.

> *(They wait. And wait.)*

> *(Lights.)*

Scene Five
Brinksmanship

[Projection: Six Months Later]

*(Lights up on **H** eating peanuts and drinking whiskey at Blue Agave Bar in Rio de Janeiro. He's a little more gray. A futbol game blares on the TV. He cracks open a deck of cards. Starts practicing some card effects. Makes a card appear. Disappear. Appear.)*

*(About now, **FRANCIS** sidles up behind him. He's a little more shorn, a little more grown up since last we saw him.)*

FRANCIS. You finally got that one right.

*(**H** freezes. Looks like he's heard a ghost. Doesn't turn to **FRANCIS**.)*

Oh, my god, it's hot down here! Nice shirt. Little tight, but you always wore them too tight.

*(**FRANCIS** waits for a reaction out of **H**. But **H** just sits quietly, still not turning. Trying to suss out what this visit is. Trying to figure out his next move.)*

Me? I've had a busy, busy, busy six months.
My frequent flyer miles? Through the roof.
I just missed you at that tree house in Costa Rica.
The ranch in Argentina. Montevideo.
Blue started to give up on me, "He's just gone, Frankie."
I said, "No way. He's out there.
I've been able to think like him so far.
I just need to get ahead of him."

From the hostel in Montevideo,

I tracked you to Sao Paolo.
I thought, "Oh. He's moving his way up the coast."
I finally got a line on you in Rio.

Got on the first plane here.
Turbulence was bad, I thought I was gonna die,
but we land, somehow.
So, the first place I head is an airport bar.
For a scotch to steady my nerves.
I'm doing some card effects and this Brazilian girl
tells me she met another American, an Asian guy,
who did card tricks too.
I said, "What are the odds?
I think I'd like to meet this guy."
She started to go through her purse,
said she had your number on a match book.
I said, "Don't worry about it. I can find him."
So, I thought like you. I thought,
"What is the shittiest hotel bar I can find
with the biggest TVs?" And ended up here.

> (**FRANCIS** *waits for congratulations that don't
> come. So, he pushes on. Looks up at the television
> screens, blasting the futbol game.*)

I asked around. Covering futbol for the local paper?
Writing about the fine line between winning and losing.
How perfect for you.
So, I'll let you get back to the sad, pathetic existence
you've carved out for yourself if you *just tell me where it is*.

H. Wait, what?

FRANCIS. What do you mean, "What?" I've come for the
comic book.

H. You've come for the comic book?

FRANCIS. What are you, a fucking parakeet? Where's the
book, H?

H. Jesus Christ.

FRANCIS. What?

H. You spent all this time looking for me because you
thought *I* had it?

FRANCIS. Look. I'm jet-lagged, and I need another drink. So, I don't want to get mean –

H. Where's Mable?

FRANCIS. How should I know? She's pulled one of her disappearing acts.

H. Frankie, I gave it to her. *Six months ago.*

FRANCIS. What?

H. To give back to Blue.

FRANCIS. *(beat)* Fuck off.

H. I swear. Seriously.

> (**FRANCIS** *grabs* **H** *and wrenches his arm behind him, throws him to the floor and presses his knee into his back.*)

Ow, what the fuck are you doing?

FRANCIS. You are really starting to wear on my last nerve –

H. Have you been working out?

> (**FRANCIS** *digs his knee harder into* **H***'s back.*)

Aaargh!

FRANCIS. Do you swear you're telling the truth?

> (**FRANCIS** *wrenches* **H***'s arm and drives his knee further into his back.*)

H. Fucking ow, you're gonna break my arm!

FRANCIS. Do you swear?

H. I don't have it! I swear!

FRANCIS. On what? What do you fucking swear on?

H. On my life.

FRANCIS. On your what?

> (**FRANCIS** *twists harder.*)

H. Ow, fuck! *(beat)* It's the only thing I have left.

FRANCIS. You swear? On your life?

H. Yes!

> (**FRANCIS** *lets go of* **H**. *Reaches out his hand.* **H** *takes it and pulls himself off the ground. Rubs his*

shoulder. **FRANCIS** *gives* **H** *a good dust off.* **H** *looks down at his wrist.)*

H. *(cont.)* My watch, please?

> *(***FRANCIS*** pulls up his jacket sleeve to reveal* **H***'s watch, which he lifted. Gives it back to* **H.** **H** *puts it back on, then pats down his pockets to find other things missing.)*

> *(Holds his hand out to* **FRANCIS** *and beckons.)*

> *(One at a time,* **FRANCIS** *produces* **H***'s phone, pack of gum, and a wad of money.)*

> *(***H** *looks down at his shirt pocket.)*

H. *(cont.)* You're slipping. You missed my pen.

FRANCIS. I'm not slipping. You'll need *this* to write with it.

> *(***FRANCIS** *produces the cartridge to* **H***'s pen.)*

H. You are. You're slipping. You just spent all that time chasing me and you should've been chasing her.

> *(***H** *starts laughing. Evilly.* **FRANCIS** *goes over and grabs* **H** *by the lapels.)*

FRANCIS. Are you fucking conning me?

H. Stop-stop-stop! I swear I'm telling the truth. I was trying to give it back. You could use pliers and staple guns on me and I'd say the same thing.

FRANCIS. Why would you steal it and then give it back?

H. Mable told me –

> *(Special up on* **MABLE.** *A memory.)*

MABLE. Blue said that what hurt her is that you were a crew and you did this to her.

FRANCIS. But even the best Chinese guilt never worked on you.

H. No, but then she said –

MABLE. She said if you do this, you're dead to her.

H. And I said, "Dead like, she's not talking to me anymore? Or literally dead, like she's gonna put a hit out on me?" And she said both!

FRANCIS. But whenever you're in trouble, you just run.

H. But, then she closed the deal by saying –

MABLE. Jason Manheim is after her. She's gonna have to run. Because he wants blood.

H. *(to* **FRANCIS***)* And that was it. I gave it back. I ran so Blue wouldn't have to.

> (**MABLE** *smiles and then disappears.* **FRANCIS** *studies* **H** *and decides to believe him. For now. He releases* **H***'s lapels.)*

Is Manheim after her?

FRANCIS. No. We broke back in and put your copy in the frame. He hasn't realized it's a fake yet. You are apparently that good a fabricator.

H. Her fingerprints?

FRANCIS. We wiped the place down. Didn't leave a trace.

H. Fuck. Mable played me like a fucking Mark.

FRANCIS. *(realization)* She used the Psychological Game on you.

H. The what?

FRANCIS. Mess with The Mark's head to get them to do what you want. Blue was going to use it on you.

H. Blue?

FRANCIS. She was supposed to be the one to meet you. The stuff about breaking code? Saying you're dead to her? Blue was sure that if she pressed those buttons, you'd give her the comic back.

H. Well, she was right.

FRANCIS. I can't believe it actually worked. Wait –

> *(Special up on* **MABLE***. Another memory.)*

MABLE. I'm really proud of both of you, you know that? You work well together.

> (**MABLE** *disappears.)*

FRANCIS. Fuck! She used it on me too.

H. Wait, what?

FRANCIS. She got us, too. We crewed up to get you.

H. Mable was working with you?

FRANCIS. To steal it back. But when you didn't show up for the buy with Blue, we didn't know what happened. Mable showed up that night, like, "I have no idea why he would miss the meet." We didn't know that she'd already met you.

H. So, she stole from you too? She broke code twice!

FRANCIS. You can only break code if you're a crew. I don't know what the fuck we are.

> (**FRANCIS** *reaches for* **H**'*s drink and slugs the whole thing down.*)

We're gonna go get it back.

H. I can't.

FRANCIS. I wasn't really asking.

H. If I set foot back in the States, I'm a dead man.

FRANCIS. You're a dead man if you don't.

H. What?

FRANCIS. Like I said, Blue turned us all onto Game Theory. There's this principle called Brinksmanship. Heard of it?

H. No.

FRANCIS. They're using it now in Israel and Palestine. The president was using it with all that fiscal cliff bullshit with Congress. If there are two parties that won't budge, to get someone to cooperate, you escalate threats to *the brink* of disaster until the other guy has to back down. For instance, with you. If you don't help me find Mable, if you run, I will find you again. And I will give you to Jimmy.

H. What? Are you serious?

> (**FRANCIS** *moves to the bar and picks up* **H**'*s deck of cards.*)

FRANCIS. I am showing you my cards to save us all a lot of time. I need you to think like me. Understand how serious I am. And if you get hurt, it will be your fault.

H. My fault?

FRANCIS. With other people, I could use other methods. They call them "contract enforcing strategies."

> (**FRANCIS** *deals out three cards, face down. He flips one over and shows it to* **H.***)*

I could threaten to destroy your reputation. But you took care of that yourself.

H. Hey!

> (**FRANCIS** *puts the first card back in the deck. Flips a second card over.)*

FRANCIS. I could threaten to take all your money and bankrupt you. But I checked your bank account, and I scanned the Caymans and it looks like you're dead fucking broke and there's nothing left to take.

> (**FRANCIS** *takes the second card and puts it back in the deck.)*

So I want to show you that you have given me no other option.

H. Really? This is your only option?

> (**FRANCIS** *looks at the last remaining card. Picks it up. Contemplates it. Slowly tears it in half.)*

FRANCIS. Don't make me hurt you, H. Don't make me sidestep grifter rules and resort to violence.

H. *(beat)* You want me to conclude on my own that my only choice is to cooperate?

FRANCIS. Pretty much.

H. You guys are brutal.

> (**FRANCIS** *starts advancing towards* **H.***)*

FRANCIS. You started this. You're the only reason we're here.

H. Okay, okay. Fine.

>*(He holds out his hands in mock bondage.)*

I am your cooperative servant.

FRANCIS. Are you?

H. Yes.

FRANCIS. Good. C'mon. We have plane tickets to buy.

>*(**H** gathers up his things, leaves some money on the bar.)*

H. Nice rope.

FRANCIS. Thanks.

H. You ever miss this?

FRANCIS. Every day. Desperately.

>*(As **H** and **FRANCIS** start to head out of the bar.)*

H. So, even if we do find Mable, how do we get her to hand over the comic?

FRANCIS. Easy. We're gonna put your life on the line.

>*(Lights.)*

Scene Six
Reputation

*(On the stoop outside her Providence, Rhode Island apartment, **BLUE** smokes while cramming for a math test. **H** walks up and stands at the foot of the stairs.)*

H. Hi.

(She doesn't look up from her text book. She's memorizing formulas.)

I miss you.

BLUE. …

H. I do. I miss you, B.

(Beat. A desert lives between them.)

You must have plenty to say to me.

BLUE. …

H. Girl that I know wouldn't waste a good sucker punch. C'mon. I'll give you one good shot.

*(**H** offers his face, ripe for a great wind up and knockout.)*

I'm not gonna offer again. It's a once only deal.

*(**BLUE** turns to stare him down, hard, for a long moment.)*

BLUE. Think like a Roper. What do I want to hear right now?

H. Forgive me?

BLUE. Forgive you? God! How did you pass Mable's test? You're fucking ridiculous –

H. B –

BLUE. Not the words I'm looking for.

(She starts to leave.)

H. I was worried you were in danger.

BLUE. I was. He came here, you know? Jimmy.
  He showed up looking for the comic or the money or
  some blood.
  I told him you stole it and he laughed.
  "That brother of yours makes *me* look like a good guy."
  Then he said, "How 'bout I hold you ransom?"
  I said, "Don't waste your time.
  You think if he ran out on me, he's gonna come back?
  To save me?"
  So he left. Because he realized I wasn't worth anything
  at all. To you.

H. That's not true. Didn't Francis tell you what happened?
  I tried to give it back.

BLUE. Well, I didn't get it, did I? I'm late for my midterm.

    (*She starts to bolt with her backpack. When she's
    almost gone –*)

H. You always wanted to know how I got home. From
  Staten Island.

    (*She turns.*)

BLUE. Well?

H. (*beat*) I took a cab.

BLUE. You what?

H. Took me awhile. To flag one down. In Staten Island.
  Ten-year-old Chinese kid by the side of the road.

BLUE. So why did they pick you up?

H. I had a fifty in my shoe.

BLUE. Why?

H. The same reason I always had all my baseball cards and
  action figures in a backpack by the door.
  Shit could go wrong at any time.
  Fire. Flood. Fucked up mom.
  I told you. Dad said you always carry Disappear Money.
  Just in case you have to disappear.
  I know I gave you a fifty for your ninth birthday.

BLUE. You did?

H. Remember? I told you to keep it in your shoe.

BLUE. *(remembering)* Oh. Right. *(beat)* But that was before Dad disappeared. So, I didn't think you were serious.

H. So, what happened to the fifty?

BLUE. I think I bought stickers.

   (He laughs. She hits him on the arm. Hard.)

H. Ow.

BLUE. Why didn't you just tell me it was a test?

H. Then it wouldn't have been a test, would it?

   (She hits him again.)

I wanted to tell you. Mable said if I did, she'd leave you in Jersey.

BLUE. …

H. Tell me you carry it now. You carry Disappear Money now, don't you?

BLUE. …

   *(**H** takes out a wad of cash.)*

H. Are you crazy? Jesus Christ. Here –

BLUE. I don't want it –

H. Take it –

BLUE. I don't want your damned money. I want my comic back!

H. Blue –

BLUE. Why'd you do it, H? Why'd you steal from me?

H. They said they were going to kill me! I didn't plan to do it. When I woke up the morning of the job, Jimmy called and said he'd upped it to three hundred fifty grand with interest. And I had twenty-four hours to pay up.

BLUE. That's not what I'm asking.

H. Then what are you asking?

BLUE. How you could do this *to me?*

H. …

BLUE. Because I would've helped you. I would've done anything for you. Then.

H. I'm sorry, B.

   (The magic words. Finally.)

BLUE. So, you didn't plan to take it?

H. No. Last minute desperation move. I didn't even think it all the way through.

BLUE. You didn't look at me like a Mark?

H. No.

BLUE. Good. Cause I was gonna say you did a shitty job. If you planned it.

   (H *goes to hug her.)*

Yo, step off. We are not all good.

H. But –

BLUE. I'm still down the hundred grand in set up with nothing to show for it. Just hoping Jason doesn't pull out a magnifying glass and realize the original is gone.

H. Look –

BLUE. Not to mention that I'm the laughingstock of the entire industry. Girl that let *her brother* get away with the take of the decade –

H. Then, let's go get it back. Steal back what we fairly stole to begin with.

   (BLUE *considers this. Gives* **H** *the hairy eyeball.)*

BLUE. Everything you're saying and doing could be misdirection.

H. It's not.

BLUE. You're just trying to keep me from kicking the shit out of you until you can steal the comic back from Mable and go to Costa Rica.

H. I won't run.

BLUE. Of course you will.

H. Francis said you taught him about Brinksmanship.

BLUE. I did.

H. So, use that on me.

BLUE. You mean, tell you that if you run, I'll track you down like the dog that you are and give you to Jimmy.

H. That's the spirit.

BLUE. Why are you giving me the move to use on you?

H. Because I owe you. And I need you to leash me. In case I can't leash myself.

> *(beat)*

We need you to pull this off. It'll take all three of us.

> *(**BLUE** nods.)*

Could you rope her?

BLUE. Frankie is always The Roper.

H. He can't be this time. Has to be you.

BLUE. Why?

H. We have to switch up roles. If we play all the regular parts, she'll see it coming.

BLUE. You have her location?

H. Not yet. Francis has been doing some homework but she's been off the grid for awhile.

BLUE. That'll buy me some time to figure out the rope. It's gonna have to be something totally out of the box.

H. Hey…

BLUE. Yeah?

H. If we can get the comic back for you…would you consider wiping the slate clean?

BLUE. Wiping the… How about we get through this and I don't kill you?

H. I had to try. *(beat)* So. You in?

> *(Lights.)*

Scene Seven
When I Was Houdini, Or Max Malini Was My Idol

> *(New York. Lights up on* **FRANCIS** *standing in front of a modern version of Houdini's Chinese Water Torture Cell. Projection of TV coverage feed while we watch him.)*

FRANCIS. People ask me, "Why this trick? Houdini?"

No. Not Houdini.

When I was seven, I didn't know how to swim.

In fact, I was afraid of the water.

So, one summer day, at the local pool,

my mother pushed me in.

> *(Lights up on* **MABLE** *in the sports betting section of an Atlantic City Casino, watching.)*

I froze.

Sunk to the bottom of that pool like a rock.

I started choking because I was inhaling water.

By the time my brother dragged me out of the pool,

he said I looked blue.

> *(Lights up on* **H** *in a NYC dive bar, also watching the live feed.)*

That night, to cheer me up, he bought me sparklers.

He put one in my hand, said,

"How long does this thing stay lit?"

> *(Lights up on* **BLUE** *crossing the stage, her school books in hand, staring intently into her iPad. She stops and sits on the ground to watch.)*

"Count from one, Frankie."

And he lit that sparkler with the end of his cigarette, and I counted.

> *(He takes out a sparkler and lights it.)*

One... Two... Three... Four... Five... Six... Seven... Eight... Nine.

The sparkler went out.

"Frankie, when trouble goes down,

that's how long you have to make a decision.

Walk to the shallow end. Signal for rescue. Try to swim.

Something.

But, make a move. Don't sit still."

Tonight, I'm going to break the world record

by holding my breath for seventeen minutes.

All before getting these handcuffs off.

> *(He finishes locking the chains and shackles.)*

(with showmanship) Let's see how much I learned from my brother!

> *(Click. He winks at the camera and drops into the tank. The lid is closed. He starts to wriggle and stretch, trying to free himself of his bonds. **BLUE**, **H** and **MABLE** all watch, rapt. A Siri-like **VOICE** starts to announce the elapsing time, which is also projected.)*

VOICE. One minute.

H. That's not what I said, you asshole.

VOICE. Five minutes.

BLUE. It'd be really fucked up to die on TV.

VOICE. Eight minutes.

MABLE. You used to run across hot coals when you were twelve.

VOICE. Twelve minutes.

H. I said, "Make a good move." Not just any move.

VOICE. Thirteen minutes.

BLUE. You said you gave up roping to get out of danger.

VOICE. Fourteen minutes.

MABLE. You'd lock yourself in the freezer in the garage and try to break out.

VOICE. Fifteen minutes.

H. Did you ever learn how to swim?

VOICE. Sixteen minutes.

BLUE. You're the only one who's not crazy. Please don't die.

VOICE. Seventeen minutes.

MABLE. I always thought you pulled those stunts to punish me for the swimming pool. Are you still punishing me?

> (*A breathless moment.* **FRANCIS** *struggles and strains. He's not able to get the shackles off. He's drowning.*)

Oh, my god.

VOICE. Eighteen minutes.

> (*blackout*)

MABLE. Pull him out!

> (*Sirens.*)

Scene Eight
Flim Flam

(JFK Airport. **MABLE** *walks out of the terminal with her favorite purse and a rolling bag, scarf, and sunglasses on. She eyes a nervous* **BLUE** *smoking at the curb and makes a bee line towards her.)*

MABLE. Where is he? Is he dead?

*(***BLUE*** stamps out her cigarette.)*

BLUE. At Beth Israel. In surgery.

MABLE. Surgery?

BLUE. When he was trying to get the cuffs off, he was straining so hard he tore his aorta.

MABLE. Oh, my god.

BLUE. They're having to patch it.

MABLE. Jesus Christ.

*(***MABLE*** paces.)*

I swear he pulls these stunts just to spite me. He's trying to give me a heart attack.

BLUE. Right. Because it's all about you.

MABLE. I'm not in the mood for your attitude.

BLUE. My attit...whatever.

MABLE. Whatever? You whatever!

BLUE. I don't have time for your bullshit!

MABLE. I don't have time for your mouthing!

BLUE. There's more trouble, M.

MABLE. What do you mean more trouble?

BLUE. It's H.

MABLE. Goddamnit. Can't he have the good grace to put his drama on hold while your brother is in the hospital?

BLUE. H was coming back to see Francis.

MABLE. He was?

BLUE. The doctors told me to call all of you.

MABLE. It's that bad?

(BLUE *nods.*)

BLUE. Jimmy must've heard H was coming back.

MABLE. What?

BLUE. When I got here to pick him up, I saw him getting pulled into a black sedan. Jimmy said, "I'm taking him to The Dentist. He'll lean on your brother until he tells me where the comic is."

MABLE. What the fuck is this? One of my sons is in the hospital fighting for his life and the other has been taken by a psychopathic –

BLUE. I know. It's really fucked up. This family is really fucked up.

MABLE. You're sure? The Dentist has H?

BLUE. Yes. You've heard what The Dentist does.

MABLE. I have. *(beat)* I would think you'd be happy. He stole from you.

BLUE. But, he's my brother.

MABLE. …

BLUE. What if they torture him?

MABLE. Well…

BLUE. What if they *kill* him, M?

(BLUE *starts to cry.*)

MABLE. Oh, stop that. *(beat)* Seriously, stop that. Stop crying.

BLUE. But, what do we do?

MABLE. Do? What do you mean? We should go to the hospital. Francis needs us.

BLUE. H needs us.

MABLE. Don't you ever get tired of saving him?

BLUE. Yes. But somebody has to.

(BLUE *puts her hand up to hail a taxi. She fights back tears.*)

I'll drop you at the hospital.

MABLE. *(sighing)* Get me a meeting with The Dentist.

> *(**BLUE** hugs her around the waist.)*

BLUE. Thank you!

> *(**MABLE** disengages **BLUE** from the hug, grabs her by the shoulders and looks her directly in the eye.)*

MABLE. Really. You have to stop.

> *(**BLUE** nods. Takes a deep breath, pulls it together.)*

BLUE. Let's go.

> *(They exit.)*

> *(Lights.)*

Scene Nine
Securing The Exit

(Lights up on a meat locker.)

(It's icy cold. Sides of beef hang everywhere. A blue tarp has been laid down on the floor. There is a tray of dental implements, archane tools, a sawzall.)

*(**H** is bound to a vintage school desk. One arm tied to the desktop, one tied at his side. Both legs tied to the chair. He looks worse for the wear. Blood stains his shirt. His face is a mess. He's unconscious.)*

*(The door swings open and **MABLE** enters with **BLUE**. They're horrified by what they see.)*

MABLE. Henry?

*(**H** stirs. Looks up and sees **MABLE**.)*

H. Help me.

*(**FRANCIS** steps out of the shadows clothed in a white hazmat suit. There's a clear plastic face shield on his head, tipped up like a jaunty hat.)*

FRANCIS. Welcome, Mable. Blue.

MABLE. Francis?

BLUE. Oh my god.

MABLE. You're alright?

FRANCIS. I needed a meeting with you but you weren't picking up your phone. Rude, really. So, I had to figure out some way to get your attention. And here you are.

MABLE. I thought you were nearly dead.

FRANCIS. I'm not. *(indicating **H**)* But he is.

MABLE. What are you doing?

*(She swings around to look at **BLUE**.)*

I asked you to set up a meeting with The Dentist.

BLUE. I thought I did.

FRANCIS. *(to **MABLE**)* You do have the comic. Don't you?

H. *(to* **MABLE***)* Did you bring it? The comic? Tell me you brought it.

(They all scrutinize one another.)

MABLE.	FRANCIS.
What is this?	What the fuck is going on here?

BLUE. Wait. Where's The Dentist?

FRANCIS. I am The Dentist.

BLUE/MABLE. What?

MABLE. What do you think I am? Some rube off the street?

H. M, please. Give him the comic. He's going to kill me!

MABLE. Who?

H. Francis! Francis is The Dentist!

MABLE. Francis is The Dentist?

FRANCIS. Didn't I just say that?

MABLE. Even if I believed that Francis were The Dentist –

FRANCIS. I am! I *am* The Dentist!

*(***MABLE*** turns to look at* **BLUE***.)*

MABLE. What did Jimmy say to you?

BLUE. *(to* **MABLE***)* I asked him to set up a meeting with The Dentist. Just like you said. I didn't know who he was. *(to* **FRANCIS***)* What are you doing?

FRANCIS. You can have whatever's left after his debt is cleared.

BLUE. I don't want it. Not like this –

FRANCIS. *This* is the business, Blue. If you don't like getting your hands dirty, you're in the wrong business.

BLUE. How much is Jimmy paying you?

FRANCIS. It's not about the money.

MABLE. It's always about the money.

FRANCIS. I'm doing it for free.

MABLE. Why?

FRANCIS. One: He owes Blue either the comic or a lot of money –

BLUE. I told you, I don't want this –

FRANCIS. And two: I don't really like code breakers.

H. Mable broke code too! She broke code!

(FRANCIS *advances towards* MABLE.)

FRANCIS. That is true, isn't it? If he's telling the truth? You stole from H? Then stole from me and Blue. Stole from your own family?

MABLE. I don't know what you're talking about.

H. I gave her the comic to give back to Blue. And she took it. She took it!

MABLE. He's lying –

H. I told Blue to go to you because I thought… Mable… look at me…he is serious. Just give him the comic book. Please.

(MABLE *just looks at him.*)

You raised me –

MABLE. Not my choice. I liked your father. And you and Blue came with the package –

H. I'm begging you. Don't let him kill me.

MABLE. I'm sorry things have gotten so fucked up for you, Henry.

H. No, don't go! Wait!

(MABLE *starts to make for the door.*)

BLUE. Mable –

H. If you didn't come with the comic, then why did you come at all?

MABLE. I came to plead with The Dentist for your life because I thought you were in danger. But now I see it's only your brother, so I think you can handle this one yourself.

(FRANCIS *picks up the sawzall and turns it on. It makes a sick grinding noise.* MABLE *stops dead in her tracks.*)

H. Wait, what are you doing?

FRANCIS. I just need to know, Mable, if H is lying or not. He says that you have the comic. If you don't, I'm going to take him apart piece by piece. Until he tells me where it is.

MABLE. Well, I don't have it!

FRANCIS. You don't?

H. Did you sell it? Jesus Christ. Do you at least have the money? You must've cleared two mill –

MABLE. I don't have it. No comic. No money!

H. Where is it? What did you do with it?

FRANCIS. You don't have it?

MABLE. No.

FRANCIS. Well that is too bad for you, H.

>*(***FRANCIS*** puts down the face shield and holds the sawzall to ***H****'s finger.)*

H. No no no no no no! She's lying –

>*(***FRANCIS*** cuts off ***H****'s pinkie finger. Blood spurts everywhere. ***H*** howls in pain. ***FRANCIS*** reveals the severed pinkie finger.)*

>*(***MABLE*** and ***BLUE*** scream.)*

>*(***FRANCIS*** mock screams back at them. Then shoots the finger into the cooler full of ice like a free throw. He pops the face shield up.)*

MABLE. What in the fuck are you doing?

BLUE. Francis!

>*(***BLUE*** starts to run towards ***H*** but ***MABLE*** holds her back.)*

FRANCIS. I'm losing patience, H. Where's the comic?

H. *(cowering over his hand)* She has it! Oh, fuck!

FRANCIS. Yeah, I heard that last time and I don't like lies, so if you don't give me the answer I'm looking for, the next thing I cut off will be a lot more precious than that finger.

H. Mable!

BLUE. Francis, stop it!

FRANCIS. No! I'm tired of liars and cheats thinking they can run roughshod over good people, honest people –

MABLE. Stop!

FRANCIS. And tonight it ends. The lies end…

> (**FRANCIS** *picks up the sawzall and starts advancing towards* **H.**)

…or else it is the end of you.

H. I don't have it. I don't. So just kill me.

FRANCIS. Okay. If you say so…

> (**FRANCIS** *puts the face shield down and flips on the sawzall. Starts revving it like an old Mustang and goes for the next finger.*)

MABLE. Stop! Stop, I did it!

> (*They all swing around to look at* **MABLE.** **FRANCIS** *turns off the saw.*)

FRANCIS. You what?

MABLE. I took it.

FRANCIS. Why? Why did you take it?

MABLE. Because I'm dying.

> (*She wobbles. Starts to faint.* **BLUE** *goes to catch her.*)

BLUE. Mable?

MABLE. Get me a chair. I have to put my head between my knees when this happens.

> (**FRANCIS** *reluctantly releases* **H** *from his bonds and all three move her to the desk.*)

Water.

> (**BLUE** *goes to find water.* **MABLE** *puts her head between her knees and breathes deeply. All* **BLUE** *can come up with is the flask of bourbon from her purse.*)

BLUE. It's all I have.

> (**MABLE** *takes the flask and is about to drink when her eyes finally fix on* **FRANCIS**. *She suddenly snaps awake, as if remembering where she is.*)

MABLE. You.

> (*Beat.* **MABLE** *straightens herself up.*)

I'm not afraid of you.

> (**MABLE** *takes a drink.*)

H. Mable. What you said before…

MABLE. …

BLUE. Are you really dying?

MABLE. You really think I'm that fucked up? To fake dying?

H. Mable. Are you or are you not dying?

MABLE. I'll tell you if you show me your hand.

> (**H** *exchanges looks with* **FRANCIS**.)

Show. Me.

> (*Before anyone can stop him,* **H** *shows his hand. Five fingers. Fully intact.*)

FRANCIS.	**BLUE**.
What the fuck are you doing?	H!

H. I had to know!

MABLE. I am. Dying. I'm sorry, Henry.

BLUE. You are dying?

MABLE. Stage 4. Pancreatic. Radiation fucks me up. I get weak sometimes.

H. That's really fucked up.

FRANCIS. Why are you dying?

MABLE. I don't know. It's really fucked up.

BLUE. Why didn't you tell us?

MABLE. You were too busy fucking each other over. And all this…

(She waves at the tarp, the blood, the sazall.)

FRANCIS. Blue taught us this game theory gem called The Credibility of Threat and Commitment.

H. We needed a credible threat to me.

MABLE. *(to **FRANCIS**)* So, you made me believe you were The Dentist.

*(**FRANCIS** nods.)*

H. And we had to show that he was really committed to fucking me up unless you gave us the comic.

BLUE. And by the way, roping you by making you think Frankie almost died? My idea. This meat locker, The Dentist? All my idea.

H. So, can we have it back now?

MABLE. Good planning. Good execution. Shame you couldn't finish the job.

BLUE. What?

MABLE. You got me to admit I have it. But now that there's no threat, why should I tell you where it is?

(They all turn to look at her.)

FRANCIS.	**H.**
Fuck!	Goddamnit!

MABLE. Calm down. You can have it back. On one condition: Are you the crew that won't break code?

BLUE. What?

MABLE. The doctors said I had a year. If I was lucky. I was going to tell you all when I heard H stole the comic from Blue. I realized that you'd started looking at each other like Marks. That was never supposed to be. I stole the comic so you'd all hate me.

H/FRANCIS. What?

MABLE. I thought if you could work together on something, work against me, maybe… You'd find each other again. Become the crew that doesn't break code.

FRANCIS. But you let this go on for six months?

MABLE. It's not my fault you took so fucking long to find him.

FRANCIS. Hey!

BLUE. Wait. *(lightbulb)* You got us together, we worked together. You got what you wanted.

H. I think you owe us that comic, now.

MABLE. So, you are a crew? You'll always have each other's backs?

H. When you say crew, do you mean "family?"

MABLE. No, I mean crew. The comic will go to my successors. I'll give you all my contacts. You can teach her what I taught the both of you –

BLUE. Teach *me?*

FRANCIS. No, Mable, I'm still out.

H. So am I.

BLUE. I'm still in!

MABLE. *(ignoring* **BLUE***)* But don't you see how you make each other better?

H. I told you. I'm trying to make a new life.

MABLE. Francis?

FRANCIS. It's not negotiable. After this, I'm done.

MABLE. *(to* **FRANCIS** *and* **H***)* I can't believe it. All that time I spent teaching you. Wasted. Why would you squander your talents?

FRANCIS. That's what you think?

H. We aren't wasting them. We're just reappropriating them.

MABLE. To do what? Gamble badly?

H. I write about the pursuit of winning better than anyone.

MABLE. Then, why can't you ever win?

H. I'm trying to change. Why would you drag me back into this?

MABLE. *(to* **FRANCIS***)* And you. The ice pillar stunt in L.A. The water tank in Vegas. I watched those.

FRANCIS. You watched?

MABLE. Oh, I watched. And all I could think was…
"What a shame that this is what he's become. Nothing
more than a circus act."

FRANCIS. You wanna know why I do this? Because of people
like you.

MABLE. Like me?

FRANCIS. The con men that only believe
in fucking people over.
I always thought what we do could be used for good.

> (**MABLE** *snorts with laughter.* **FRANCIS** *plows
> forward.*)

Being a Roper, I learned how people think.
What they expect.
So, when doing an illusion, I ask you to look over here –

> (*He puts one hand up, shows an empty palm.*)

And you expect something to happen over here.
But instead –

> (*With the other hand, he makes a card appear out
> of nowhere.*)

I have a card appear over here.

MABLE. It's just a party trick.

FRANCIS. No, because instead of stealing something from
you, I'm giving you something.

MABLE. And what would that be?

FRANCIS. I'm expanding the limits
of what you think is possible.
Helping you see that limits aren't limits at all.
It's not just a card appearing out of nowhere.
Breaking out of a pillar of ice.
Holding my breath for seventeen minutes.
It's the impossible being possible.
It's making you think for a second,
there's nothing you can't do.

(**MABLE** *turns this over in her mind. Looks at*
FRANCIS.)

MABLE. Can I cheat death, Francis?

FRANCIS. Mable. Anything is possible.

(**MABLE** *is almost swept up by this for a second.
But, then –*)

MABLE. But, it's not. I'm going to die, Francis. And I taught
you so that you would carry on when I'm gone. Now
what will I have to show for it? The Kwan family name
dies with me.

BLUE. You should've taught me. They didn't even want it. I
wanted it. *(beat)* But I didn't pass your test.

BLUE. You left a young girl at The Rockaways.

MABLE. …

BLUE. You never even asked how I got home.

MABLE. …

BLUE. Do you know where I slept? Under some stairs on
the Lower East Side. The whole time I was thinking,
"She doesn't even know where I am. I could be dead
for all she knows."

MABLE. *(finally)* Did anybody hurt you?

BLUE. And if they had? Why didn't you ask me then?

MABLE. …

BLUE. You remember what you finally said to me when I
got there? "Come Inside." That's it.

MABLE. …

BLUE. It's like you wanted me to fail.

MABLE. I did.

BLUE. What?

MABLE. So you wouldn't get into this profession. It's a shitty
field for women.

BLUE. Any field is a shitty field for women.

MABLE. I didn't want you to do some of the things I've had
to do.

BLUE. Maybe I wouldn't have to. I've learned everything there is to know about the con –

MABLE. *(not exactly)* Well –

BLUE. And I have game theory –

MABLE. Still.

BLUE. I have the intangibles. Maybe I'm smarter in ways you can't see.

MABLE. Can't you see it's not about how smart you are?

BLUE. Of course it is.

MABLE. I was preparing you for the worst. Out of all of you, *you* were the least prepared.

BLUE. What?

MABLE. You were always so sunny and trusting. It used to really piss me off. You used to smile too much. I had to tell you, "This is New York. All that smiling will get you in trouble."

BLUE. My smiling pissed you off?

MABLE. Because I used to be like that. Until I couldn't be anymore. Until too many things had happened. You need armor or people will take advantage of you.

BLUE. What happened to you?

MABLE. No one told me how awful people can be. They're your friend one minute and don't know your name the next. *Everyone* is on the make. And if you don't develop the strength to withstand their betrayals and rejections and disappearances, you will be crushed underfoot –

> *(Winded and pained, she is cut short. **BLUE** hands her the flask and she takes a long pull. **H** tries to comfort her by putting a hand on her shoulder, but she shakes it off.)*

BLUE. Why didn't you just say that?

MABLE. That you learn by living through things. Resilience. You learn that by surviving. You may think I was hard. But if you survived me, you can survive anything. *(beat)* You can all thank me later.

FRANCIS. Thank you?

H. I'll never thank you for that.

BLUE. I'll do it. Thank you.

FRANCIS. Why are you thanking her?

BLUE. Because I'm not just going to survive. I'm going to be better than *(to* **MABLE***)* you, *(to* **FRANCIS***)* you and *(to* **H***)* definitely you.

H. Hey!

BLUE. So, thank you for the preparation.

>　　　(**MABLE** *nods to her.*)

You said the comic goes to your successor. So, that's me. They're out, but give it to me.

FRANCIS. You promised me this was the last one.

BLUE. But, I can't see myself doing anything else. I don't want to be doing anything else.

FRANCIS. That's not enough.

BLUE. What if this is my magic?

FRANCIS. That would mean using what you know for *good.*

>　　　(*Lightbulb.*)

BLUE. I can do that.

FRANCIS. How?

BLUE. It's not about the money. I just want to stay in the game. I can steal things back and return them to their rightful owners.

H. Interesting. There'd be a huge market for that –

FRANCIS. Don't encourage her –

BLUE. Maybe I can get paid to right wrongs.

FRANCIS. B –

BLUE. I'd start with returning the comic to Manheim.

H. Are you fucking kidding me? We need to sell it so I can square away with Jimmy.

BLUE. I could always use a good Fixer.

H. You know what he'll do to me if he finds me?

> (**H** *waves at the entire room – the torture ephemera,
> blood, meat locker, sawzall –)*

This. And that's just for starters.

BLUE. Then keep your head down. Long enough to help
me run some jobs. We'll rack up enough to pay down
your debt.

H. Who's gonna hire us? Your reputation's still in the
shitter, no offense, and I'm a code breaker.

MABLE. You only ever need one big score to put you back
on the map.

BLUE. Show them what we're capable of. And I bet you,
we'll have more jobs than we can handle.

H. Steal from thieves? Grift from grifters? You realize how
crazy this sounds.

BLUE. Do you want to be on the run forever? Or do you
want your life back? Your call.

H. I can't believe I'm even considering this.

FRANCIS. *(to* BLUE*)* I didn't give you enough credit. I see
what you're doing.

BLUE. What am I doing?

FRANCIS. Running three simultaneous cons. You're roping
H to be your Fixer. You're conning me into releasing
you from our agreement. And you're talking Mable
into letting you be her successor.

BLUE. *(to* MABLE*)* Is it working?

> (**MABLE** *walks over and picks up her purse. She
> reaches in and reveals none other than* Action
> Comics #1.)*

H. You had it in your purse the whole time?

> (**BLUE** *reaches for the comic but* **MABLE** *holds it
> away from her.)*

MABLE. Are you prepared enough?

BLUE. Yes.

MABLE. Will you be able to watch your back? I won't be there.

BLUE. I'll be fine.

MABLE. How will I know that?

BLUE. Come watch me run a job. You'll see.

> (**BLUE** *reaches for the comic again, but* **MABLE** *holds it further away.*)

MABLE. Not so fast. This'll be payment for your first job.

BLUE. Which is what?

MABLE. If you can pull this one off? You'll be hired to do anything.

BLUE. What. Do. You. Want?

MABLE. I've always wanted to touch "Starry Night."

H. Touch it?

MABLE. When I was a girl, my father and I snuck into MoMA. I thought the swirls and the stars were so beautiful, I just wanted to touch them. So I reached out, to feel those swirls, but the guard stopped me. I threw such a tantrum, they threw me out. I swore one day I'd be back. And I'd touch that painting.

FRANCIS. You want them to break into MoMA? *(beat)* That'd take at least a grand slam.

H. Four simultaneous cons? I think it'd be more like five or six.

MABLE. Probably the Sweetheart Con, The Spanish Prisoner, The Wire –

FRANCIS. God, I love The Wire.

BLUE. That'd take at least six months of planning.

MABLE. I probably don't have that. We'd have to work faster.

BLUE. *(to* **H***)* We could do it.

H. Maybe. Three-man crew? I think we need one more.

> (*They all turn to look at* **FRANCIS***.*)

BLUE. Frankie?

FRANCIS. No.

BLUE. C'mon, we're not stealing anything –

FRANCIS. No, no, no, no no.

MABLE. It's your dying mother's wish.

FRANCIS. I hate all of you. *(to* **MABLE***)* You just want to touch "Starry Night?"

MABLE. Yes, just a touch.

FRANCIS. Nothing funny.

MABLE. No. Nothing funny. Just a touch and Blue can have the comic back.

FRANCIS. Jesus, fine. One last score.

H. I've always wanted to be The Lure. Can I be The Lure?

FRANCIS. How are you gonna be The Lure?

H. Watch and learn, Frankie.

*(***FRANCIS*** just shakes his head.)*

FRANCIS. I can be The Fixer.

MABLE/BLUE. I'm Inside Man.

(Beat. Uh-oh.)

I'm Inside Man.

*(It's a stalemate. ***BLUE*** puts out a fist for Rock-Paper-Scissors. ***MABLE*** smiles. Follows suit.)*

MABLE. Okay, Belinda Kwan. Let's see how good you really are.

BLUE. On "Go." One-Two-Three –

(Blackout.)

End of Play